Firstly, I want to thank you for buying this book.

Secondly, I want to thank everyone who has helped me so much long the way, my Dad for reading through it first and persuading me to add three extra chapters. Then thanks go to my Mum for doing the first couple of proof reading sessions and to James, my brother, who helped me come up with some of the teacher's names and for me to bounce ideas off.

I also mustn't forget all the friends I sent it to for them to check I was on the right track. Finally, my thanks go to Tim and Annette Hughes. Tim has helped me through the publishing process, and Annette has provided all the illustrations.

I hope you enjoy reading my story which is the first of four in my Magic Meg series of books

ABOUT ME

At primary school I had a big group of friends, but when I left and started to use a wheelchair, a lot of those friendships disappeared so most of my friends are now adults. At secondary school when it came time for me to do my GCSE's some of the teachers didn't believe that I could cope with doing exams, but I was quietly determined to prove them wrong. Also I am organised, I can prioritise work and I have a lot of will-power.

My hobbies are reading books mostly centred around animals. I've also got on my bookshelf children's classics which include Black Beauty, Heidi and The Secret Garden. I love horse riding, I'm part of the RDA and I've competed in competitions and won some rosettes. I like to watch Disney, Pixar and Dreamworks films, I also like the old comedies which include Are You Being Served, Bewitched and Open All Hour.

All profits from the sale of this book will go to the AT Society who have helped us so much.

Magic Meg Goes to School

Meg's Family

Mr Morris   Mrs Morris   Megan   Billy & Bobby   Tamsin   Izzy

The Main Characters

Mrs Grim- Bocker   Mrs Brimstone   Miss Britle- Bottom   Mr Silver- screen   Mr Stradivarus   Mr Black

CHAPTER 1

All about Meg

Hi, my name's Meg, it's really Megan Morris but everyone calls me Meg for short. I'm a witch, but not a very good one,

I daren't tell the rest of my family because they're all so good, I'm scared what they'll say if I tell them. Anyway I better introduce them to you before you die of curiosity.

First off there's Dad, he's a GREAT wizard (he was a straight A student in school) but he likes to try and live like an everyday 'run of the mill' normal mortal person (not that I've seen a normal one you're all so different).

He doesn't always stick to it though. I've caught him many times when he comes home from work doing magic for simple things like putting on his slippers or getting his newspaper. He works as a solicitor because he says, "It's a job a normal person does."

Right that's enough about Dad on to Mum.

My Mum is a good witch, but not as good as my Dad, but no-one in the magical world is. Mum doesn't work (oops sorry, I mean she looks after the house!) although she used to be a teacher and looking after us is lots of hard work.

She says proudly,

"It is certainly hard enough and keeps me busy but it's the most important job I'll ever do" which I think is really sweet.

Mum specialises in household magic, (thinking about it I bet all mortals wish they could do housework using magic!). The things I've seen are unbelievable, but they soon will be believable because I'm going to tell you about them.

I've seen hoovers pushing themselves and when they're finished downstairs they float upstairs, dusters dusting for themselves, washing up doing itself and clothes jumping up sorting themselves out and going into the washing machine.

But Mum goes out herself to peg out the washing because she doesn't want anyone to know we're a magical family. Now for my little brothers or 'little terrors' as I call them!!!

There's two of them, as if one of them wasn't enough! I nick-named them 'Double Trouble', but their real names are Billy and Bobby, and they're twins, they're too young to do magic but that doesn't stop them trying.

This is quite useful sometimes like when I try a spell and it goes wrong - I can just blame it on them. It also means I don't have to tell my parents I mucked up yet again.

I tell you what it's a good job they can't talk yet otherwise they would have told on me ages ago. (Oops, I almost forgot to tell you how old everyone is!!).
Well I'm 9 years old and my parents always kept that quiet because they were scared someone from the authorities would come to try to make them enrol me in school but mainly they worried whether there'd be a school left at the end of the day.

Then there's my parents, well I don't know exactly how old they are because grown-ups never talk about age do they?

All I get if I ask Mum is,

"I'm as old as my tongue and a little older than my teeth"

and my Dad says,

"It's too personal,"

Which, as far as he is concerned, almost everything is too personal.

Lastly there's my young twin brothers who are both 18 months.

Finally I better explain where we live. We live in a normal street in a normal town with normal neighbours, but we are not a normal family we have magic, but Mum and Dad won't let me do magic outside the house.

"Pretend you're a normal person," they say

I have no idea why, but I do it anyway just to please them.

CHAPTER 2

Meg enrols in school

One day, early in the morning, I was in my room with my two little brothers Billy and Bobby, (it wouldn't have been so early if they hadn't woken me up at seven o'clock and once they're awake there's no question of anyone sleeping!). I was trying to keep them out of mischief, which is easier said than done. The doorbell rang and I went on the landing to see what was going on. I let Mum and Dad deal with what was going on downstairs, my hands were full with looking after the little terrors upstairs.

They opened the door and a stout, average height, serious looking lady dressed in a tweed skirt and jacket with a smart white blouse and a big black hat met their eyes.

My parents, having very good manners, invited her in (not only for this reason but also because she looked so stern and cross they didn't know what she was going to do or say next and if you're like us you don't want any unwanted attention). When she was safely indoors she announced that she was Mrs Grimshaw from the Education Services and they had noticed that their oldest daughter hadn't enrolled in school yet.

At this point good manners went out of the window for Mum and Dad and they didn't even offer their unwelcome guest a seat. Mum immediately asked Mrs Grimshaw how she knew this at which point Mrs Grimshaw stood up to her full height, threw back her head so both Mum and Dad could see up her nostrils and in quite a snooty and threatening voice she said,

"We have ways of knowing these things Mrs Morris."

As Mum and Dad remarked afterwards - she said it in a way a bit like a spy.

Mrs Grimshaw carried on talking and gave an ultimatum.

"We expect your daughter to be at school within the week."
With that she turned around on her heels and strode out the door.

Mum and Dad said "Goodbye" after her, but she was already well out of sight.

CHAPTER 3

Meg's first day at school

The next morning I woke up to the sound of Mum calling to me from downstairs to get dressed and come down, she and Dad wanted to talk to me. I got dressed in some very old, tattered jeans and a plush pink top and hurried downstairs to see what all the hubbub was about. Mum ushered me into the kitchen where Dad was sat on his chair at the breakfast table with a place beside him for Mum. Billy and Bobby the twins were sat at the head of the table in two matching highchairs, (Mum says that's so she's not showing favouritism, but how are they going to know at 18 months?) Dad and Mum were eating breakfast, well I say eating, it was more like trying to eat, the twins were gurgling and making their porridge magically fly up and land in each other's faces!

When I came in everyone stopped what they were doing - even the twins, which I thought was weird because normally they don't take any notice of anything. I felt like a condemned person as I sat down on the opposite side of the kitchen table to Mum and Dad.

Mum sat down, opened her mouth to speak and said,

"Meg we had a lady come round yesterday who said you have to start school, so I have found you a place at a school called 'St Bridget's School of Learning'. It's just down the street and they said as today is Friday you can come in your own clothes and get your uniform tomorrow in town."

When she had finished I looked at Mum and then Dad in turn thinking what to say, and then I said,

"Why can't you teach me here because then you can teach me magic too?"

Dad piped up at this point and said,

"Of course we could but it doesn't work like that in this mortal world we live in".

So that was the end of that conversation.

After breakfast Mum took me to 'St Bridget's School of Learning'.

When we arrived at the gates and we opened them they made a loud creaking noise like someone needed to oil them. I thought to myself if someone hadn't bothered to oil a gate I wasn't going to like it here and they definitely weren't going to like me. As we walked through we came into a big green space with white lines on it like a football field. We looked beyond the field and saw the big imposing school building. (Well I say building - it was more like buildings - there was a huge, tall building in the middle and two long rectangle shaped ones either side of it).

When we got to the massive oak doors a tall thin lady answered. She was wearing a black jacket and skirt with a white blouse. On her feet were high heeled shoes which were bright red, the same shade as her lipstick and on her long, bony, bird beak nose was a pair of matching red glasses. Her hair was done up in a tight bun.

She stood at the door and in a very shrill voice, she said,

"Hello you two, I've been expecting you. I got your Mum's call late last night to say our school was gaining another student. All the other students are in lessons at the moment, but it will soon be break time, so you can stay out here while your Mum and I sort some of the paperwork in my office. My name's Mrs Grim-Bocker and I'm headmistress here."

So Mum went off with Mrs Grim-Bocker and left me outside alone. I found a bench. There were four of them altogether, neatly spaced outside the school buildings, and on either side of the benches were two trees. I wasn't sat there long before the bell rang and all the children rushed out of the door and onto the field. Well most of them did except two, one girl was wearing glasses and the other girl was in a wheelchair. I think they were friends because the girl with glasses was pushing the girl in the wheelchair. They went over to one of the benches.

After a bit a boy peeled himself off from the rest of the group on the field and came over with his own gang, by the look of him I suspected he was a bit of a bully. When he arrived at the bench he took the glasses off the girl sat on the bench and started playing catch with them with two members of his gang, while she tried to run after them. Meanwhile another two members of the gang were making fun of the girl in the wheelchair.

I had had enough of this so I decided to cast a spell to give them continuous farts. Dad had told me once that people like that bully are very insecure. So I decided that was a good spell to do because they'd be embarrassed and run away, which of course they did. As I was casting the spell on the bully and his gang, the girl in the wheelchair looked around and saw me muttering under my breath. Once the bully and his gang had run off she told the other girl what she had seen and they came over to speak to me. As they approached I said,

"Hello, my name is Megan but everyone calls me Meg, what are your names?"

The girl in the glasses spoke first,

"My names Tamsin,"

The girl in the wheelchair then spoke,

"My name's Izzy."

Izzy went on to say,

"You know when those bullies had farts continuously, were you the one to give them those by magic?"

I replied,

"No I didn't" and then added

"Why do you say that?"

Izzy said,

"Well for quite a number of reasons really.

One: I've never seen anybody fart continuously before.

Two: I saw you muttering under your breath.

Three: you were really concentrating, and while everyone was laughing you just looked relieved

Four: I've never seen it come out in green clouds before."

I then replied,

"How do you know its magic?"

To which she said,

"I read books on witchcraft, are you a witch then?"
I thought for a minute. They seemed like really nice girls and they looked as if they needed a friend as much as I did. So I told them that I was, but they had to keep it a secret. They both crossed their hearts and promised not to tell. I thought I've done well for myself, it's not been 5 minutes yet and I've already made two friends for myself.

CHAPTER 4

Meg the scientist

After break Mrs Grim-Bocker called me into her office. When I arrived she was sitting in one of those big, black office chairs that I always think look like fun to play in. She was turned away from me when I opened the door but when I entered the room she twirled around as if she had a sixth sense. She got straight to the point and said,

"I'm going to get you to do a normal school day. Your first lesson of the day is science. I have assigned to you two students Tamsin and Izzy, just so you don't feel like you're thrown in at the deep end without a float."

I knew what she meant because Dad had mentioned the phrase before in one of his chats.

"I informed them before you came in this morning" and with that she dismissed me out of her office.

As I walked along the long corridor with Izzy and Tamsin, Tamsin looked at me. She saw I was scared so she said to me,

"Don't worry the teachers aren't as scary as Mrs Grim-Bocker. The science teacher, Mrs Brimstone, she's just crazy".

I then said,

"What is it with all the teachers in this school having scary names?"

"That's because they're trying to scare us before teaching us." Izzy replied.

When we arrived in the science class-room we found a long, low table big enough for the three of us to sit alongside each other, in the middle of the room, in front of the white boards. The rest of the children were sat on stools behind tall tables, with more tall tables going at right angles to them. The tables had weird tube endings which were covered with blue lids. When I asked Tamsin what they were she said they were used to pump gas in but there were levers on them to shut them off. I instantly had visions of the teachers gassing us if we got too naughty.

The teacher walked in and she certainly lived up to the term 'crazy'. She looked like a female version of those 'mad scientists' you see on TV. Her hair was white and looked like she'd just put her finger in a light socket. She wore a white coat that hung down to her ankles and it was buttoned up to the top, so no one knew what she was wearing underneath. She had one of those necklaces you hang glasses on, except hers was made of rope, and she had bare feet. When she got to the white board she stopped, picked up a pen and wrote her name on the board. She turned towards the class and spoke in a half SHOUT, half giggle in a really deep voice.

"Good morning class, we have a new person joining our class, and her name is Megan Morris. Today, we will be dissecting frogs."

With that she picked up a bunch of dead frogs in a bag and started to pass them round the tables. As soon as we got ours I immediately started to think about frogs and before I knew it, even without me saying a spell, where Mrs Brimstone had stood, there was a FROG! All the children burst out laughing, I turned round to Tamsin and Izzy mortified and said,

"What am I going to do?

I JUST TURNED A TEACHER INTO A FROG!"

"Don't worry Meg no one's going to tell on you. For one thing they don't know it was you and we've got a rule if something funny happens in the class-room nobody talks about it except if it's about

bullying or something bad happens"

Tamsin said quite calmly, as if this was something that happened every day.

Izzy added,

"Yeah and you're young. The spell won't last for that long, just put her outside on the grass."

So I did and I guess she's ok, because I saw her an hour later and the only weird thing was that she was chasing flies!

CHAPTER 5

Meg the artist

I hoped what happened in that lesson was a one off, but unfortunately it was one in a long line of mishaps. Anyway the next lesson of the day was art with a lady called Miss Bristle-Bottom. While me, Tamsin and Izzy were making our way down the corridor towards the arts class-room, I said to Tamsin,

"Is this art teacher as crazy as she sounds?"

To this Tamsin answered,

"Not really crazy just 'airy fairy'"

and Izzy added,

"Yeah and make sure you listen to the way she talks; she's got a very strong accent."

When we arrived at the class-room and went inside there were eight tables all together, but they were put together in pairs to seat four people. On the tables there were long thin jars with a selection of paint brushes and pens in them, and these were in the middle of each table.

Like me, Tamsin and Izzy found a place to sit on the front row.

"Why do you always have to sit at the front?" I asked Izzy.

To this she replied,

"One because it's easier for me to see the board and two it's easier for me to get in and out the class-room."

When the teacher came in, she was wearing a white linen shirt and trouser set, a floaty jacket thing that came down to her knees and her hair was auburn and had a purple head band holding it up. The colours of the jacket were like one of those rainbows you get when oil is spilt on the pavement.

As she crossed to her desk and started the lesson she said,

"Today we are going to be learning about Vincent Van Gogh"

She then asked one of the children to hand out textbooks.

When the textbooks had all been handed out, Mrs Bristle-Bottom instructed us to turn to page 32 and read up on Vincent Van Gogh while she popped out for 5 minutes to see a delivery guy about some paints.

As she left the class-room we got our heads down to some serious reading, after all the section on Vincent was 10 pages long. I had been reading for a while and just got to the bit where Vincent got into a fight with another painter. How he had an illness that caused him to have seizures and he had found a knife.

I looked up to stretch my neck and standing there in front of me was VINCENT VAN GOGH with his ear still attached.

He stood there totally perplexed and a little bit stunned by his sudden time-travelling experience, I thought to myself that I must have brought him back before 1888 because that was the year they think it all happened (saying that I don't know how they know that, but it's in all the books so it must be true).

I elbowed Tamsin who looked up and then managed to attract Izzy's attention. Miraculously the rest of the class were still concentrating on reading their books. When the young Vincent had regained his composure he asked,

Où suis-je et comment suis-je arrivé ici?"
To which I replied,

"Right then Mr Van Gogh I think you are asking 'Where am I and how did I get here?'

I can explain the first bit of that question, you are in a class-room,

in a school."

To which he replied, "Je ne comprends?"

Then I proceeded to try and explain, and I said,

"Well school is a building where people go to acquire knowledge and class-rooms are rooms inside the building."

But I forgot he was French so he couldn't understand a word I was saying, I immediately turned to Tamsin who looked at Izzy who wheeled round in her chair and

translated all I was saying into French. Tamsin leaned over and whispered to me,

"She's half French, I think she said her Mum was French, that's why she's so fluent."

So after all that was explained we set about trying to change history. We explained to the young Vincent about what all the history books said would happen to him.

"No matter how mad you get or how bad things seem to be anything's better than cutting bits off yourself. Also keep all sharp objects like knifes locked away in a safe place," I said.

After I said this I asked Izzy to translate it all into French so Vincent could understand it. Then as we finished talking to him he began to slowly vanish. As we heard Miss Bristle- Bottom's footsteps coming down the corridor he vanished totally, which was quite handy. Amazingly the rest of the class still had their heads buried in their books all of that time (I thought they were all just asleep). After class had finished we stayed behind for a bit to look at the pages about Vincent Van Gogh. Our little talk must have worked because the information on the pages had changed in the meantime.

CHAPTER 6

Meg the actress

After we left the art class-room, I turned to Tamsin while she was wheeling Izzy down the corridor and said,

"What's the next lesson?"

To which Tamsin replied,

"It's Drama".

"What's this teacher like?" I asked.

Izzy immediately piped up,

"He's very fashionable and dramatic"

"Isn't he supposed to be? He is teaching drama after all," I said.
"Yes but he over-dramatizes everything the way he speaks, dresses and moves," Izzy replied.

When we got to the class-room, it was a big room surrounded by curtains a bit like it was a big stage. In the centre of the room there were tables set up in a U shape. We sat in the middle of them and everyone else sat around us. The door suddenly swung open and posing in it was our teacher. Then he said in a very sweet voice,

"I'm now here my darlings."

He tossed his head back and swaggered to the front of the class-room. Izzy was quite right he was "fashionable." He was wearing a pink neck tie, yellow sun glasses (even though we were inside), matching white linen jacket and trouser set and slip-on shoes. As he reached the front of the class he stopped, turned, put his hand on his hip and gestured with the other.

"Hello, my little artists, my name is Mr Silver-Screen and today we will be submerging ourselves in Shakespeare. I will give you a brief explanation of his play 'Romeo and Juliet', and you will then split yourself into groups and perform your own renditions," he said.

So as Tamsin and Izzy were my two best friends (my only friends in fact and as they knew about my magic, I picked them). As soon as we started talking and deciding on what we were going to do, my mind was full of Shakespeare. All of a sudden I noticed Mr Silver-Screen had disappeared and in his place was none other than WILLIAM SHAKESPEARE.

He stood there a bit stunned. As he was still slowly recovering, I turned to Tamsin and Izzy and said worriedly,

"If Shakespeare's here where is Mr Silver-Screen?"

Very quickly Izzy replied,

"Simple, Mr Silver-Screen is where Shakespeare was, so he'll be in the Tudor era"

Izzy could see I was still worried and added,

"Don't worry when the spell wears off both Shakespeare and Mr Silver-Screen will switch back with each other, and Mr Silver-screen won't remember a thing".

When Shakespeare had regained his composure, he asked all sorts of questions. Where was he and how he had got there? I had to concentrate very hard because he spoke in old English, 'theeing' and 'thouing' all over the place. He wore a very tight green velvet tunic, white tights and black shoes with silver buckles in the middle. He was aghast at the idea that girls were allowed to act (which they weren't allowed to do in Tudor times). Once he knew that we were doing 'Romeo and Juliet' he became very interested and wondered why we weren't sticking to the proper plot. We tried to explain that we had to adapt it, but all he said in response to that was it was perfect before so why change it?

But luckily before he could argue any further the spell slowly wore off and he disappeared. He was replaced with Mr Silver-Screen who immediately swooned as he arrived back in reality. Being a drama teacher I thought that he would have liked being in The Globe theatre.

CHAPTER 7

Meg the musician

We picked Mr Silver-Screen off the floor and helped him into a chair to recover from his recent trip! The bell went and it was time for the next lesson, which I was reliably informed was music with Mr Stradivarius.

We walked (and wheeled) down to the class-room and went in, it was an amazing sight, all around the edge of the room was every instrument you could possibly think of (and probably some you wouldn't). Also there was a big black grand piano in the middle of the room, with chairs set up in front of it in rows like in the theatre.

All the others had sat down as we wheeled Izzy to the front row and parked her on the end next to us. After talking amongst ourselves, Mr Stradivarius appeared in the doorway and strode across the class-room.

He was dressed all in black, his jacket was embroidered with red thread and round his neck he wore a big swirling cape.

As he got to the middle of the class-room he sat down at the piano and turned the stool round towards us.

He said in an Italian accent.

"Good afternoon children, I am Mr Stradivarius and as my name is musical I thought I better explain it to you. A Stradivarius is one of the violins, it was built by members of the Italian family Stradivari, particularly by Antonio Stradivari during the 17th and 18th centuries."

As soon as he had finished, my head was full of everything he had just told us and suddenly there in Mr Stradivarius's place was a magically floating violin. When the violin appeared there must have been an overflow of magic from it because all the instruments jumped up and started playing by themselves.

They were of course playing some kind of Italian music. It was great FUN with everyone up dancing, even Izzy was having a bop in her wheelchair and swinging her arms in every direction.

But as before after a while the spell wore off and everything went back too normal.

Well as normal as you can have with magic!

CHAPTER 8

Meg the historian

It was soon time for home. I decided not to worry Mum and Dad and just pretended that everything was fine at school.

So that's what I did, when Mum and Dad asked me how school was, I said,

"It's still there"

and ran upstairs to play with Billy and Bobby.

Next day everything went normally until we got to history in the afternoon. When we went into the class-room it was in complete darkness, apart from candles dotted around the outside of the room.

We found a table long enough to seat three of us so I could sit by Tamsin and Izzy.

When the teacher walked in he was wearing a black suit under which he wore a white shirt and a black tie, his hair was grey with a bald patch in the middle.

When he spoke his voice came out in one constant dull tone that sounded like he was bored himself. He said,

"Good afternoon class, my name is Mr Black and today we are going to be studying dinosaurs."

While Mr Black wrote his name on the black board I whispered to Tamsin and Izzy,

"I can see why he's called Mr Black he wears Black, he's surrounded by Blackness and his voice even sounds Black."

"Yes" replied Tamsin "and his favourite period in history is the Black Death which is dead depressing like his

personality, but he's a good history teacher if you don't fall asleep," she said with a laugh.

Then he turned and started the lesson. As soon as Mr Black started talking about Dinosaurs I started thinking about them and although I'm not sure how it happened but as by now you have come to expect MR BLACK TURNED INTO A DINOSAUR.

Of course all the class thought this was hilarious, all except for the bully (who had finally returned to school after the day I zapped him and he'd run away). At this point I wanted to learn why the bully was the way he was, so I asked Tamsin and Izzy. Tamsin said,

"Well, he's called Barry and when he started school he used to be bullied himself".

Izzy then added,

"Yes, and as he got older he got fed up of being on the receiving end and became a bully himself and surrounded himself with big strapping boys to protect him."

Then after a bit she added,

"Now I think about it he must be very insecure, self-conscious and not happy in himself so he makes everyone miserable like himself".

But I shouldn't have worried about him telling on me, because the Dinosaur (or should, I say Mr Black) took one look at Barry and ATE HIM.

Poor boy - but maybe everyone gets their come uppance!

CHAPTER 9

Meg in trouble

Everyone ran out of the class-room screaming, including me and Tamsin pushing Izzy (she usually propelled herself but this time she made an exception). We stopped when we thought that we were far enough away to be safe, and started to chat about what had happened. I began to get worried.

At this point Izzy saw the expression on my face and tried to calm me down.

"Don't worry nobody liked Barry anyway and if your spell lasts as little as last time, you'll be fine, but look on the bright side your magic must be really powerful," she said.

Then Tamsin added,

"Yeah and remember what I said last time. Students don't tell on other students if something funny happens." (funny as in something you laugh at not funny as in something odd)

However as the afternoon went on Mr Black stayed a Dinosaur and Barry still hadn't reappeared. It just kept getting worse, because at the start of every lesson they take a register and the teachers thought it strange that Barry wasn't there as he had been there earlier, so they reported it to Mrs Grim-Bocker.

I was then immediately summoned to Mrs Grim-Bocker's office. As I entered she swung round in her big black chair like she had done on my first day. All she needed now was a white cat to stroke and she could be a villain in a James Bond film. Dad enjoys them so I know all about them. As I thought about this I smiled but when Mrs Grim Bocker saw the look on my face she immediately started shouting shrilly,

"STOP SMILING GIRL!!! Do you know what you've done? Now because of you we've got to report a missing person to the police and inform the parents."

She seemed to totally have disregarded the magic side of things, perhaps she didn't understand my magic powers but even so she said,

"To protect the school I am going to have to exclude you from school."

Well that's a good start to my school career!

CHAPTER 10

Meg tries to better herself

Mrs Grim Bocker of course wanted to call in my parents to explain to them in person, but I managed to persuade her not to do that.

"Mom is taking the twins to see their Grandma today, so she is out".

She said she would be in touch tomorrow.

So after saying goodbye to Tamsin and Izzy, I started slowly walking back home, trying to decide what to say to Mum and Dad. As I reached the door I decided the best thing to do was to be honest about the whole thing, so when I opened the door, the scene played out like this.

Mum was sat in the living-room with Billy and Bobby playing on the floor. Dad though was at work which was a good thing because he would probably have hit the roof, seeing how it was his idea in the first place for me to make sure that I should seem as normal as possible and go to school. I told Mum the whole story and after I had explained it all to her, she said,

"Well then Meg, don't worry I think you'd better go up to your room and I'll explain it later to your Dad."

I love Mum she's so understanding, I love Dad too, but he can be a bit too serious on some things. As I was going up the stairs I thought I would go to Dad's study to borrow some books to study in my room. I guessed that Dad would try to get me into another school, which it turned out he did (but more about that later).

Anyway when I had got a science book from Dad's study, I went to my room and shut the door. After reading for a bit I came across a part on gravity which said, 'There is no gravity in space, therefore everything that isn't fixed floats.'

As quick as a flash without me saying a word everything started lifting off the floor. Shelves, my bed, the twins cot, wardrobe, chest of drawers, tables, and chairs. When I looked up and saw all my bedroom stuff floating about me, I rushed to my door opened it, went through and shut it again to stop anything getting out. While I was on the landing I looked downstairs, everyone was still where they were when I went upstairs, except Billy and Bobby who were floating up off the floor, flapping their arms pretending to be birds. Mum had fallen asleep in the armchair; this was floating like everything else and raised up off the floor with Mum still asleep amazingly.

When I'd seen what was going on downstairs I went back to my room to try to study, which I hoped would make the spell wear off quicker if I concentrated on something else.

As the clock struck 6 o'clock Dad came home. As Dad came through the door I came downstairs because I guessed he would want to have a chat after finding out about what had happened at school, which he did. When me and Mum had explained everything, after putting Billy and Bobby to bed, Dad straight away said,

"We must enrol Meg in another school right away,"

as Mum guessed he would.

But as she explained what had happened earlier that afternoon at home, he seemed to go off that idea. However one question remained, WHAT WERE WE GOING TO DO WITH ME?

CHAPTER 11

Meg makes her mind up

Next day I asked Mum and Dad if Tamsin and Izzy could come round. They were hesitant at first but as soon as I had explained that they knew about me and my powers and that they wouldn't tell anyone, Mum and Dad agreed and said they could come. Well mainly Mum did but Dad wanted to study mortals more closely so he agreed.

When Tamsin and Izzy arrived I answered the door and lead them into the living room and as they entered I introduced them to Mum and Dad. We thought it might be pushing our luck for them to meet the twins so we left them in their room playing.

When I'd introduced them both to Tamsin and Izzy and vice versa, Mum said,

"We are so pleased that Meg has made two friends like you" Tamsin replied,

"We made friends on the first day after Meg helped us with something" and she left it at that very tactfully.
Then when we had spoken for a bit, I asked Mum if me, Tamsin and Izzy could go into the garden and have a chat. I suggested it because I didn't want to subject Izzy to anymore of Dad studying her wheelchair. As we went through the house towards the back garden, I apologized to Izzy and said,

"Sorry about Dad, he's never seen a wheelchair before up close."

To which Izzy replied,

"That's ok I'm used to it by now, it's what happens when you are a bit 'different'."

When we got into the garden Tamsin and I sat down on our table and chair set that we had to sit out in the garden in the summer and Izzy sat opposite us in her wheelchair.

We chatted about general things for a bit and then I told them everything that had happened and I asked for their advice. They said that everything had returned to normal in the classroom and Barry the bully had been put back to normal.

After a short pause Tamsin said,

"As for what to do next - well you've got three choices, you can try to be readmitted to our school, enrol in another school or you can find a way to stay at home."

Izzy added "But if I were you I would cut my losses and make the best of it,"

After we had finished a bit more chatting they said their goodbyes and left.

Later I told Mum and Dad what they had said to me. Of course Dad wanted to enrol me in another school, but after he had thought about it he soon agreed with Mum that it should be my decision. So I had a big decision to make and I didn't know what to do.

CHAPTER 12

Meg's friends help her to
find her true self

Next day I decided, after much thought, that Izzy was right and I should make the best of a bad job. I didn't think school really suited me and if I went to another one I might blow it up or something. Now don't get any ideas about me bunking off school, the only reason I'm not going to school is because I really can't seem to control my magic.

When I got dressed I headed downstairs where I found Mum in the kitchen alone preparing breakfast. The twins were still fast asleep which was a good thing, because if they were they were awake eggs and bacon would be flying all around the kitchen.And probably some would land on me and Mum.

As I walked in I asked Mum if I could talk to her, she could sense it was important. She stopped what she was doing, and turning to me she said,

"Yes darling what is it?"

I started to explain what I was thinking about last night, how I didn't think that I was suited to school at the moment and explained why.

Mum agreed with it.

After a brief pause Mum said,

"But won't that infuriating woman come from the council to make us enrol you in another school, how will we stop that from happening?"

To which I replied,

"Oh I already thought of that, just ring the council and convince them it would be too much trouble to get me into school again. You can tell them that you're qualified to teach me here instead and Dad has a book on every subject under the sun so we should be sorted."

Then I suddenly thought about what Dad would say to which Mum said,

"Don't you worry I'll deal with your father,"

which I think she meant not to tell him. I went back up to my room to wait for things to calm down.

When Mum had explained things to Dad and it was safe to come downstairs again I came back down into the kitchen where I saw Dad sat at the head of the table with his nose buried in the paper, which he held in front of his face and he had a cup of tea by him. Mum was still trying to perfect the cooking of bacon and eggs; she'd nailed making tea ages ago.

I walked over to her.

"Don't worry I explained to Dad and he's calmed down now, I said at the end of the day it was your choice," she said with her arm around me.

I sat down at the table waiting for breakfast I thought to myself,

"Well what on earth shall I do now?"

CHAPTER 13

Meg makes her final decision

I was awake at the start of the next night thinking about what to do. Finally I decided what to do as my clock on my bedside table showed midnight. After that I settled down to try and get some sleep.

Next morning I bounded out of bed and ran downstairs. As I got down to the living room a strange sight met my eyes, Mum and Dad were sat on two big armchairs waiting to talk to me. I instantly knew why they were there so I sat down.

Mum started first and said,

"After our talk yesterday I rang Mrs Grimshaw at the Council and managed to persuade her it wasn't a good idea for you to go back to the school which eventually she agreed with and I said to her you would be home schooled and that we're qualified to teach you"

To this Dad added,

"Okay if you're not going to school, what are you going to do with all your spare time?"

As he said this I thought to myself Dad's taking this well, normally he hits the roof at stuff like this.

I think he must of thought it would be harder to appear normal if I had accidently blown up a school or something. Then I explained the thoughts to them that I'd had last night and said,

"I think I should write a book about the events and challenges that face me every day with my uncontrollable magic skills. Don't worry though the way I shall write will make sure no-one will guess we are the people in it and I'll still keep studying all the school subjects if Dad lets me borrow his books."

I said this because I knew that Dad would be worried about us having our privacy invaded but then Dad asked a question I never expected him to ask.

"But how will people know that it is all made up?" said Dad.

"Let's face it no sane person would really believe it," I replied.

Of course my friends, the only two people that knew it was all true were Tamsin and Izzy, who I am still great friends with.

THE END

Printed in Great Britain
by Amazon